Tree Song

By Tiffany Stone

Art by Holly Hatam

annick press
toronto + berkeley

We acknowledge the support of the Canada Council for the Arts and the Ontario Arts Council, and the participation of the Government of Canada/la participation du gouvernement du Canada for our publishing activities.

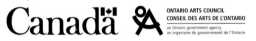

Cataloging in Publication data

Stone, Tiffany, 1967-, author
    Tree song / Tiffany Stone ; Holly Hatam, illustrator.

Issued in print and electronic formats.
ISBN 978-1-77321-001-8 (hardcover).--ISBN 978-1-77321-000-1 (softcover).--ISBN 978-1-77321-003-2 (PDF).--ISBN 978-1-77321-002-5 (HTML)

    1. Trees--Life cycles--Juvenile literature. I. Hatam, Holly, illustrator II. Title.

QK475.8.S755 2018   j582.16   C2017-905598-4
                                                   C2017-905599-2

Published in the U.S.A. by Annick Press (U.S.) Ltd.
Distributed in Canada by University of Toronto Press.
Distributed in the U.S.A. by Publishers Group West.

Printed in China

www.annickpress.com
www.tiffanystone.ca
www.hollyhatam.com

Also available in e-book format.
Please visit www.annicpress.com/ebooks.html for more details.

To my husband, Carman, for patiently waiting . . .
waiting . . . and to Kallie George for helping me
get to TA-DA!
—T.S.

Dedicated to my distracting and tree-hugging
little boy, who was no help in illustrating
this book.
—H.H.

Hushhhhhhhhhhhh warns wind
and whirls seed down.

Seed lies, silent, on the ground.

Oh-so quiet, not a peep.
Seed escapes a hungry beak.

All around thrums forest noise.
Should seed try its brand-new voice?

Twitter. Trickle.
Rustle. Growl.

Is it time yet?
No, not now.

Song of sunshine.
Song of rain.
Chirrrrrrrrrrrp!
A bird is foiled again.

Waiting . . .
Waiting . . .

Pushhhhhhhhhhhhh, TA-DA!
Seed sprouts, sings out *tree-tra-la!*

Roots reach deep and branches high,
s-t-r-e-t-c-h-i-n-g up to tickle sky.

Tee-hee-hee! Sky laughs along
as tree grows singing loud and strong.

Tree sings with the seasons too.
Summer hums in brightest blue.

Tree sings back a song of shade,
a dappled shadow serenade.

Fall calls out for fancy dress.
Shall we dance?
Tree answers *yes!*

The forest swirls red, yellow, brown.

Then
        flitter
            flutter

leaves fall down.

In winter, tree stands
bare and bold,
listens closely to the cold.

The whisper-song of falling snow,
icicles sighing as they grow.
Quiet sparkles everywhere . . .

. . . till spring rings through the frozen air.

Buds burst in a melody
of tender green
on springtime tree.

And birds, who would
have eaten seed,
come to build their
nests in tree.

An ax's *thwack*
is almost heard
but tree shouts *STOP!*
without a word.

The man looks up
and understands.
He drops the ax
that's in his hands.

So it goes, year after year.
New voices join.
Some disappear.

Tree keeps singing, on and on.
But even trees must end their songs.

Hushhhhhhhhhhhh
soothes wind eventually,
whirling round the ancient tree.

Tree sings out one final sound.

CR–R–R–A–A–A–CK!

Tree lies, silent, on the ground.

Song of sunshine,
song of rain . . .

Tree-tra-la begins again.